For Rogan
and Alex
M. K.

For Loveday
R. A.

Published by
PEACHTREE PUBLISHERS
1700 Chattahoochee Avenue
Atlanta, Georgia 30318-2112
www.peachtree-online.com

First published in Great Britain in 2004 by Hodder Children's Books

Illustrations created in pen and ink, watercolor, and a little bit of pencil crayon for the
hats and socks

Printed in China
10 9 8 7 6 5 4 3 2 1
First Edition

Library of Congress Cataloging-in-Publication Data

Kelly, Mij.
  One more sheep / written by Mij Kelly ; illustrated by Russell Ayto.
  -- 1st ed.
     p. cm.
  Summary: Sam's sheep must find a way to keep him awake
long enough to count them, so that he will not open the door
to let in what he thinks is a stray sheep, but might be an
enemy in disguise.
  ISBN 1-56145-378-1
  [1. Sheep--Fiction. 2. Counting--Fiction. 3. Sleep--
Fiction. 4.Humorous stories. 5. Stories in
rhyme.]   I. Ayto, Russell, ill.
  II. Title.
  PZ8.3.K2985One 2006
  [E]--dc22   2006006641

One More Sheep

Written by Mij Kelly

Illustrated by Russell Ayto

PEACHTREE

ATLANTA

On a wild, windy night,
in a fierce thunderstorm,
Sam brought home his sheep
and tucked them up warm,
woolly socks on their feet,
woolly hats on their heads.
They were all safe and snug
in their big cozy bed.

Now Sam owned ten sheep
and he had to be sure
that he'd brought them all in
from the wet, windy moor,
where the hungry wolf growls,
and the hungry wolf prowls,
and on wild, windy nights
the hungry wolf howls.

Sam just had to know
they were all safe in bed.
And the one way to know
was to count each mutton-head.

He counted out loud...

 **"One...**

two...

three...

four..."

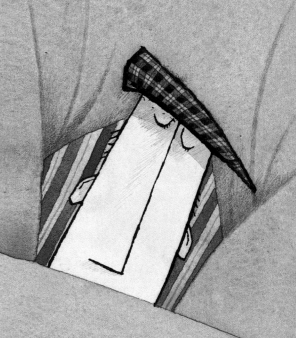

That's as far as he got before he started to snore.

"He always does that!"

"It's not that hard to count sheep!"

"Is there something about us that puts him to sleep?"

Out on the moor,
the wind whistled and wuthered,
while the sheep safe indoors
snuggled under the covers,
drifting through dreams...

'til a loud
rat-a-tat
woke them all up.

"Who is there?"
"What was that?"

Sam ran down the stairs
and threw open the door.
"Well, bless my pajamas!
It's one sheep more.
Don't stand there shivering,
Come inside! Come get warm.
What a fool I have been
to leave you out in the storm."

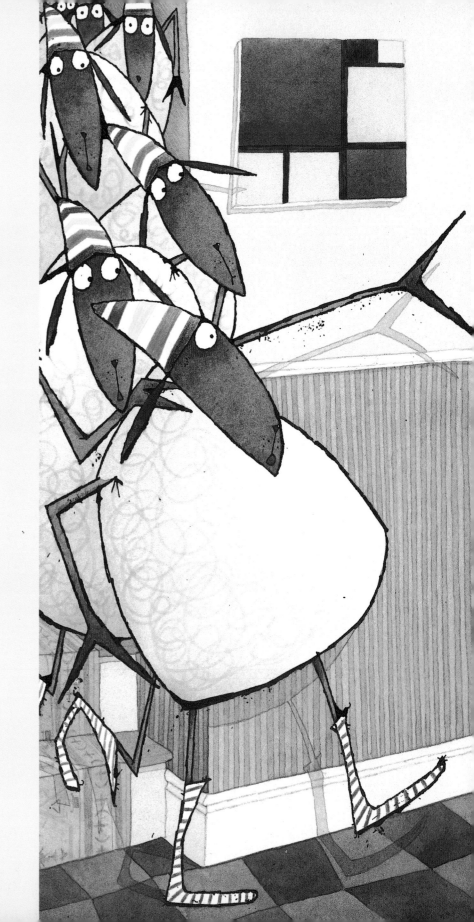

Sam said, "Don't mess around.
Remember who's boss.
Let the precious lambkin in
before I get cross."

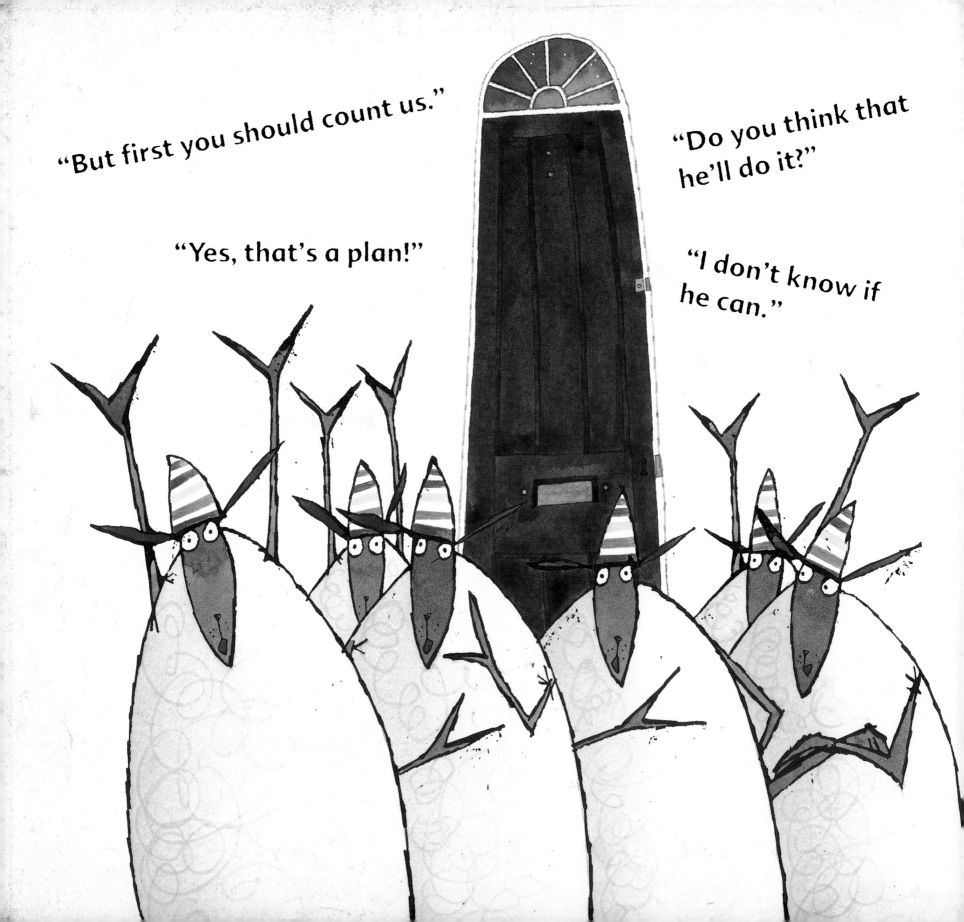

Well, Sam could count fingers
and Sam could count toes.
But he couldn't count the sheep
right in front of his nose.
He thought and he wondered.
Just what could he say?
He couldn't tell them nicely,
but he told them anyway.

"It's a well-known fact
that when people count sheep,
it tires us all out
and puts us to sleep.

You're not at all interesting.
You're not at all odd.
You're a first-class ticket
to the Land of Nod."

"Well, thanks very much!"

"How ill-mannered!"

"How rude!"

"You've got an appalling attitude!"

But boring or not,
the sheep could sense danger
they did not want Sam
to let in the stranger.

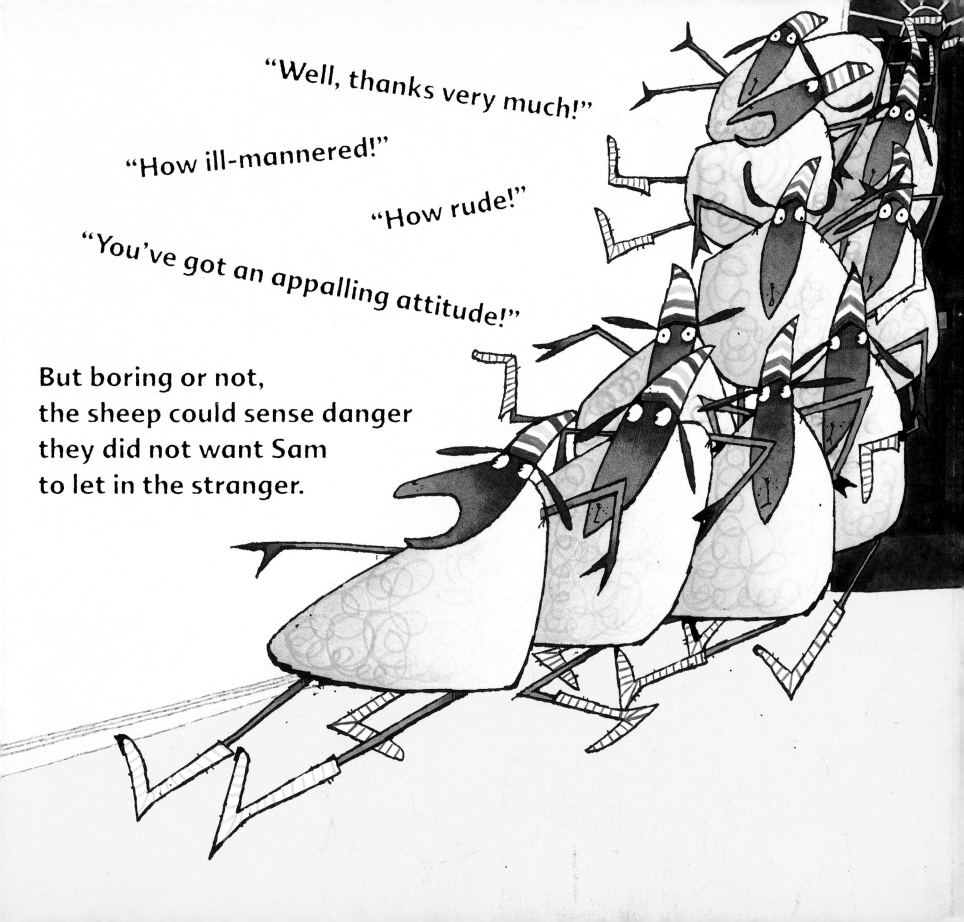

"Who," Sam cried,
"can this be then?"

And he quickly slammed the door again.

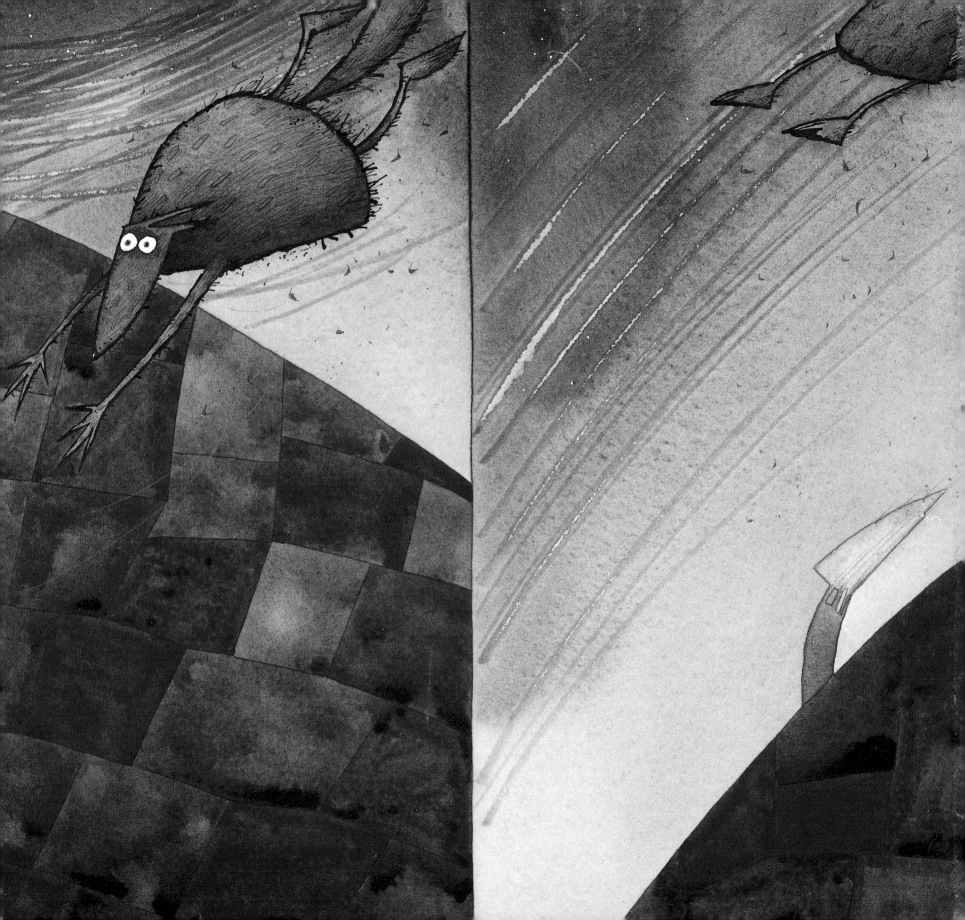

After all that fuss and fluster
Sam couldn't get to sleep,
'til he settled down and closed his eyes
and counted his boring sheep...